MW00649134

# On a Hot Day

by Mitchell James
illustrated by Anna Godwin

SCHOOL PUBLISHERS

Printed in the United States of America

ISBN-10: 0-15-351330-6
ISBN-13: 978-0-15-351330-5

Ordering Options
ISBN-10: 0-15-351211-3 (Grade 1 Advanced Collection)
ISBN-13: 978-0-15-351211-7 (Grade 1 Advanced Collection)
ISBN-10: 0-15-358036-4 (package of 5)
ISBN-13: 978-0-15-358036-9 (package of 5)

3 4 5 6 7 8 9 10   179   15 14 13 12 11 10 09 08

It was a very hot day in the city. My mom said she would take me to the swimming pool because it was a good place to cool down.

My big sister sat by a fan. The fan was blowing cool air on her, which felt nicer than the heat.

"We're going to the swimming pool," I called loudly.

"I'll come, too," she said.

We walked down the street,
side by side. I pulled my sun hat
down farther to keep the hot sun
off my nose.

We came to Jake's house. Jake's
family was sitting in the shade under
a tree.

4

"Where are you going?" Jake
called loudly.

"To the swimming pool," I said.

"We'll come, too," said Jake's dad.

We sat in the shade of their tree
until Jake and his family got their
swimming things.

5

We walked on down our street.
We saw Mr. Chin cleaning his
brown van with water from a hose.

"Hello, Mr. Chin," I called. "We're
going to the swimming pool."

6

"I'll come, too," said Mr. Chin. He turned off the hose. We waited by his van until he got his swimming things.

"It's too hot to walk," Mr. Chin said when he came back. "We can go in my van."

Mr. Chin drove us to the pool
in his nice, cool van. Everyone had
lots of fun.

I love my street. People are
friends, and they help one another.

8